W9-BIP-427

WITHDRAWN

A Gift of The Friends of The
Saint Paul Public Library

The Friends organization
acknowledges the generous support
of the John F. and Myrtle V. Briggs
Charitable Trust

Disney's
Christmas Stories

Including *Donald Duck's Christmas Tree, Santa's Toy Shop,*
Mickey's Christmas Carol

Disney's Christmas Stories

Including *Donald Duck's Christmas Tree, Santa's Toy Shop, Mickey's Christmas Carol*

A GOLDEN BOOK • NEW YORK

Western Publishing Company, Inc., Racine, Wisconsin 53404

© 1989 The Walt Disney Company. Stories and illustrations in this book previously copyrighted © 1983, 1954, 1950 The Walt Disney Company. All rights reserved. Printed in the U.S.A. No part of this book may be reproduced or copied in any form without written permission from the copyright owner. GOLDEN, GOLDEN & DESIGN, A GOLDEN BOOK, and A GOLDEN TREASURY are trademarks of Western Publishing Company, Inc. Library of Congress Catalog Card Number: 89-84575 ISBN: 0-307-15750-4/ISBN: 0-307-65750-7 (lib. bdg.)

A B C D E F G H I J K L M

Donald Duck's
Christmas Tree

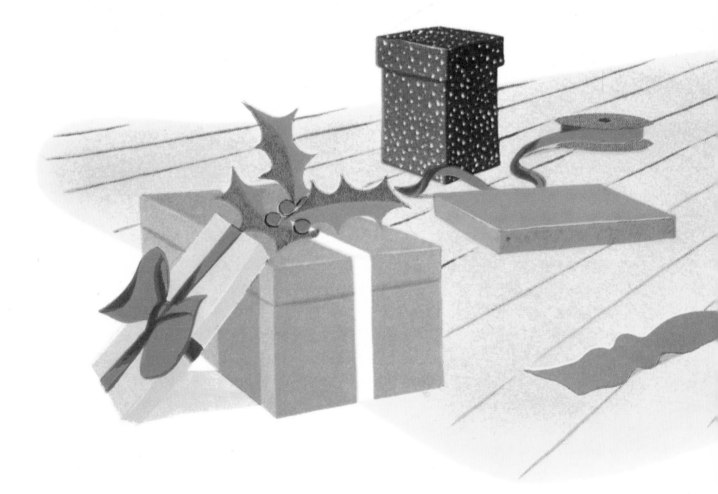

It was the day before Christmas.

At Donald Duck's house the cookies were all baked.
The presents were all wrapped. Now it was time for the
Christmas tree.

Donald put on his coat and cap and mittens. He picked up his sharp, shiny ax.

"Come along, Pluto," he called. "We're going to the woods to find our Christmas tree."

Pluto came on the run, and off they went into the snowy woods.

Now, deep in those woods in a sturdy fir tree lived two merry chipmunks, Chip 'n' Dale.

They were getting ready for Christmas, too. They had found a tiny fir tree standing in the snow near their own sturdy home. They were trimming it with berries and chains of dry grass when Donald and Pluto came along.

The chipmunks heard Donald come whistling
through the woods. Then they saw Pluto prancing at his
side. They scampered home to safety. At least, they
thought that they were safe.

But what was this? While Pluto Pup went sniffing about, Donald circled the sturdy fir tree, measuring it with his eye.

"This is just the tree for us," Donald said. And Pluto Pup agreed.

So Donald went to work with his sharp, shiny ax.
Chop, chop, chop, chop, chop!
Poor Chip 'n' Dale! Hidden in the treetop, they were
too frightened to think.

Chop, chop, chop went Donald Duck's ax. Then
creak, creak, creak went the trunk.
"TIMBER!" cried Donald, and down came the tree,
with Chip 'n' Dale clinging for dear life.

"Come on, Pluto," called Donald. "Let's take our tree home."

So home through the woods went Donald Duck, whistling as he tramped along, dragging the fir tree.

And in the branches sat Chip 'n' Dale, having a very nice ride.

Donald set up the tree in his living room as soon as he got home.

"There," he said. "Now we will trim our tree."

Donald brought out boxes of ornaments.

From their hiding place up in the branches,
Chip 'n' Dale looked on.
   They watched Donald loop long strings of colored
lights over the branches of the tree.

They watched him hang bright-colored balls—gold and red and blue. And Pluto Pup helped where he could.

"There!" said Donald when the job was done. "Doesn't that look fine?"

"Bow-wow!" said Pluto proudly.

And it was indeed a beautiful Christmas tree.

"Now I'll pile the presents under the tree for Mickey and Minnie and the rest," said Donald. "You stay here."

"Bow-wow!" said Pluto. And he sat down to admire the Christmas tree.

As soon as Donald was out of sight Chip 'n' Dale
appeared.
They danced on the branches till the needles
quivered.

"Grrr," growled Pluto disapprovingly.

But Chip 'n' Dale did not care. Chip just picked off a shiny ball and threw it at Pluto Pup!

Pluto caught it in his paws.

"Grrr!" he growled crossly again.

Then Dale picked off a ball and threw it at Pluto, too! Pluto jumped and barely caught it in his teeth. Just then in came Donald Duck.

"Pluto!" he cried. "Bad dog!" He thought Pluto had been snatching balls from the tree.

Poor Pluto! He lifted the branches, but not a sign of Chip or Dale could he see.

"Now, be good," said Donald, "while I bring in the rest of the presents."

So away went Donald again.

No sooner was Donald out of sight than Chip 'n' Dale appeared.

Out they came, dancing down the branches, those naughty young chipmunks.

Plunk! Chip's head went through a colored ball. Dale laughed and laughed at the funny sight Chip made, dancing with a big round golden head.

But Pluto did not think it was funny at all. They were going to spoil Donald's tree!

"Grrr!" he growled. But they did not stop. So Pluto got set to jump.

"Pluto!" cried Donald Duck from the doorway. "What is the matter with you? Do you want to ruin the tree?"

Of course, Chip 'n' Dale were safely out of sight, so poor Pluto could not explain.

"You'll have to go out to your doghouse for the rest of Christmas Eve," said Donald.

At that moment there was a loud crash.

"What was that?" cried Donald.

"Bow-wow!" said Pluto, pointing to the tree.
The colored lights were flickering on and off.

"What's this?" cried Donald Duck.

"Bow-wow!" cried Pluto, pointing again. Donald peered among the branches until he spied Chip 'n' Dale.

"Well, well," he said, chuckling, as he lifted them down. "So you're the mischief-makers. And to think I blamed poor Pluto Pup. I'm sorry, Pluto, boy."

Pluto marched to the kitchen door and held it open. Chip 'n' Dale, he felt, should go out in the snow.

"Oh, Pluto!" cried Donald. "It's Christmas Eve. We must be kind to everyone. The spirit of Christmas is love, you know."

So Pluto made friends with Chip 'n' Dale. They said they were sorry, in chipmunk talk. And when Mickey and Minnie and Goofy came along, caroling, they all agreed that this was by far their happiest Christmas Eve.

Santa's Toy Shop

Way up north in the land of ice and snow stands a cozy little house. And beside the front door hangs a neat little sign. "S. Claus," says the sign, because that is who lives there—Santa Claus.

Mrs. Claus lives there, too, of course. She keeps
house for Santa Claus, and for all the elves who work in
Santa's toy shop.
  And what a busy place that toy shop is!

In the doll department...

and dozens of departments up and down the halls,
happy little Christmas elves are busy all year long,
making and trying out the toys.

Oh, everyone is busy in Santa's toy shop. But Santa Claus is busiest of all. He shows the doll makers how to paint on smiles.

"I'll take a day off soon," says Santa Claus, "and play!"

But letters keep coming from boys and girls, wanting talking dolls and cowboy boots, rocking horses and fire fighter suits.

"I'm just *too* busy!" Santa Claus sometimes says. "I never have time to play with the toys."

But most of those children have been so good, Santa has to do his best to please them.

So the days whiz by in Santa's toy shop. It is almost Christmas Eve again, and Santa Claus has still not played with a single toy!

"Oh, jumping jacks!" says Santa Claus on Christmas
Eve as Mrs. Claus buttons up his warm red coat. "Now
I have to give all these toys away, and I never will get to
try any out!"

But Mrs. Claus whispers something in Santa's ear,
and he leaves the house, chuckling to himself.

"Wonderful idea!" the reindeer hear him say as they wait at the door, hitched to the heaped-up sleigh.

Then all night long around the world they fly. And
Santa drops down chimneys with his load of toys,

or slips in doors or windows, when he can't
fit in the chimneys.

The load grows lighter in the sleigh as they go. And at last Santa Claus is slipping down the chimney into the very last house on his list.

There he finds a Christmas tree all set up. He puts the
final touches on it and turns on the lights.

He finds a plate of cookies and a glass of milk with a note that says, "For Dear Santa Claus." So he sits down and has a bite to eat.

Then he unpacks the toys, as he always does. But he does not hurry. Not this time. No!

He sets up the new electric train and sends it speeding
around the track and through the tunnel.

He sends the model airplane spinning around the
Christmas tree. And he builds a whole village with
Christmas blocks.

When Santa is finished trying every Christmas toy,
back home he flies in his magical sleigh to Mrs. Claus.

"Oh, what fun I had!" Santa tells Mrs. Claus. "I stopped at the last house and played with all the toys. And I'll do it again next year!"

Mickey's Christmas Carol

Poor Bob Cratchit! Mr. Scrooge had made him work late again—even though it was Christmas Eve. But now, at last, he could go home. "Merry Christmas!" he called.

"Christmas, bah!" shouted Scrooge. "Don't forget to take my laundry."

Bob lugged the heavy laundry bag through the icy
streets. He stopped once to rest, but only for a moment.
When he thought of his family waiting for him, he
picked up the bundle and trudged on.

"It's Papa!" cried Tiny Tim joyfully as Bob struggled through the door.

"Dinner will be ready soon, dear," said Mrs. Cratchit as she put some scraps into a pan. "I wish Mr. Scrooge would pay you more.... He certainly has enough money."

But Scrooge *never* thought he had enough money. Tonight, as always, he had stayed late at the office to count his gold coins.

His nephew, Fred, opened the door.

"Here's a holly wreath for you, Uncle," he said. "I've come to invite you to Christmas dinner. We're having roast goose and plum pudding and candied fruits and—"

"Out of my way, boy," shouted Scrooge. "You know
I can't eat that stuff!"

"Give a penny for the poor?" asked a man out on
the street.

"Give *that* to the poor!" cried Scrooge angrily,
shoving the wreath over the man's head.

"All this Christmas fuss," muttered Scrooge. "Bah, humbug." He thought of his old, dead partner, Jacob Marley. "Marley never gave anything away," he said. "He was my kind of man."

Scrooge shivered. He couldn't wait to get inside his warm house.

As soon as he was indoors, Scrooge sank into his favorite chair. He was just dozing off when—

CLANK, CLANK, CLANK.

Scrooge sat up with a start. The ghost of Jacob Marley was coming toward him, slowly dragging long, heavy chains.

"I must carry these chains through eternity," moaned Marley, "because I was selfish. Your punishment will be the same, Ebenezer Scrooge."

"No!" said Scrooge. "It can't be. Help me, Jacob."

"Tonight," said Marley, "three spirits will visit you. Listen to them, or your chains will be heavier than mine."

The ghost vanished. Scrooge blinked and shook his head. "I need rest," he thought. "Imagine—thinking I saw old Marley!" He climbed into bed.

He had barely fallen asleep when the alarm clock jangled. Scrooge opened his eyes and saw a dapper little fellow standing on the night table.

"I am the Ghost of Christmas Past," he said.

The ghost held out his hand. "Hold on," he said. "I'll
take you to a Christmas of long ago."
Scrooge felt himself drift toward the ceiling. "Oh, oh,
OHH!" he shouted as they sailed out the window.

They flew across the night sky and landed near a house filled with music and cheerful voices. Scrooge looked in the window.

"Why, that's *me*," he gasped, "when I was young. And there's old Fezziwig. He gave me my first job. And there's my lovely Isabel."

"See how happy you were then, Scrooge," said the ghost. "You were full of love. But then you grew greedy and lost all your friends—even Isabel."

Scrooge turned away. "I don't want to see any more. Please, Spirit, take me home."

Ring! Ring! It was the alarm clock again. Scrooge
opened his eyes. "I must have been dreaming," he said.
"Fee, fi, fo, fum!" boomed a voice. Across the room,
a giant was sitting in Scrooge's chair, surrounded by
bowls and platters of luscious-looking food.

"What's all this?" demanded Scrooge.

"It's the food of generosity," said the giant, "something you know nothing about. I'm the Ghost of Christmas Present. Come and see what's happening tonight." He picked Scrooge up and dropped him into his deep pocket.

Outside, the giant set Scrooge down in front of a tiny tumbledown house. Scrooge peered through a cracked window. "It's the Cratchits!" he said. "What a measly dinner they're having. Why aren't they eating the food in the bubbling pot?"

"That's your laundry," said the giant. "They're boiling it to make sure it gets extra clean."

"What's wrong with the lad?" asked Scrooge.

"Tiny Tim is very ill," said the giant. "He needs good food to make him strong and well. You should pay his father more so he can buy his family enough to eat...." The giant's voice faded, and then he was gone.

Scrooge tried to call the giant back, but it was too late. Suddenly he was surrounded by thick clouds of smoke. When the air cleared, he was standing near a broken-down tombstone in a shadowy graveyard.

"Hello, Scrooge," said a voice behind him. "I am the Ghost of Christmas Future."

Scrooge turned to the ghost. "Whose lonely grave is this?" he asked.

"See for yourself," said the ghost. "It belongs to a man who was very rich. But he was so selfish and unkind that he had no friends."

Scrooge bent to read the name on the stone.
"Ebenezer...Scrooge. Oh, no! This is *my* grave!"
"That's right!" The ghost laughed.
"No, please," begged Scrooge. "I don't want to die all
alone, with no friends. I'll change my ways, I promise!

"I'll change..." Scrooge's eyes flew open. He was in his own bed. He was still alive—and there was still time to change, to make a new beginning.

"It's Christmas morning!" he cried. He dressed quickly and rushed outside.

"Take these!" he called, tossing bags of money to the men collecting for the poor.

"Hello, Fred!" he shouted when he saw his nephew. "May I still come to dinner?"

"Of course, Uncle," replied Fred.

"Splendid! I'll see you later. There's something I must do first."

A while later Scrooge knocked at Bob Cratchit's door.

"Merry Christmas!" Scrooge said happily. "I have another bundle for you."

"M-more laundry, sir?" stammered Bob.

Scrooge laughed. "Don't be silly, my boy!"

"Look, Papa," cried Tiny Tim, opening the sack. "Toys!"

"Friends are worth more than all the gold in the world," said Scrooge. "Cratchit, from now on you and your family will have all the good food and warm clothing you need. Merry Christmas, my friends!"

"And God bless us everyone!" shouted Tiny Tim.